for Alfie

© 2001 by Michael Neugebauer Verlag,
an imprint of Nord-Süd Verlag AG, Gossau Zürich, Switzerland
First published in Switzerland under the title *Theodor Terror*.

First published in the United States, Great Britain, Canada,
Australia, and New Zealand in 2001 by North-South Books,
an imprint of Nord-Süd Verlag AG, Gossau Zürich, Switzerland.
Distributed in the United States by North-South Books Inc., New York.

Library of Congress Cataloging-in-Publication Data is available.
A CIP catalogue record for this book is available from The British Library.
ISBN 0-7358-1476-7 (trade binding) 10 9 8 7 6 5 4 3 2 1
ISBN 0-7358-1477-5 (library binding) 10 9 8 7 6 5 4 3 2 1
Printed in Italy

For more information about our books, and the authors and artists
who create them, visit our web site: www.northsouth.com

Beneath the trees something was stirring—something really scary!

Its nose twitched and wrinkled as it sniffed about.

Rumbles and gurgles rose from its belly like thunder.

It was hungry—*really* hungry, and it could smell something yummy. . . .

Deep in the forest it was lunchtime.

All the animals were busy cooking and the air was filled with delicious smells.

Old Mole sat in his kitchen and licked his whiskery lips.

"Mmmmm . . . yummmm . . . burnt toast. How I love it!" he said.

But before he could take a bite, a terrifying sound from outside made his whiskers stand on end.

"aaaaaa . . . aaaaaaa . . . tschoooooooooo!"

Old Mole ran to the window to see what it was and almost jumped out of his skin with fright.

For there, sitting in his garden, was a DRAGON !

"Oh, no!" cried Old Mole in alarm.

"It's Jasper the Terror!"

Dragons love toast more than anything in the world.

Particularly if it's burnt toast.

"I say," said Jasper the Terror in his little squeaky voice, "is that toast I smell—*burnt* toast?"

Before Old Mole could utter a word, Jasper the Terror's nose began to twitch . . .

"aaaaaa . . . **aaaaaaa . . .**"

"Look out!" screamed Old Mole. But it was too late.

Jasper was unhappy.

Every time he sneezed he set fire to something—trousers, shoes, stray cats. . . .

He couldn't control his flame, and now everyone ran away and hid whenever he appeared.

They hid their trousers.

They hid their shoes.

They called him "terror."

"Jasper the Terror!"

The very next day all the animals held a meeting.

Trouserless, they gathered beneath a grumpy oak.

"What can we do?" they asked one another.

They scratched their heads.

They looked in books.

They wrote things down on little pieces of paper.

But nobody knew what to do.

The next time Jasper came looking for toast he got a terrible shock.

Nailed to the grumpy oak was a sign that read:

NO DRAGONS ALLOWED!

(Particularly dragons called Jasper!)

Poor Jasper hardly had time to read his name before his nose began to twitch again. . . .

"aaaaaa . . . aaaaaaa . . . tschoooooooooo!"

Flames roared from Jasper's nose and set fire to the sign.

"Oooops," said Jasper quietly.

Now, it wasn't that nobody liked Jasper. Everybody *loved* him.

But when it came to losing your trousers, well . . .

Jasper soon found himself all alone in the forest.

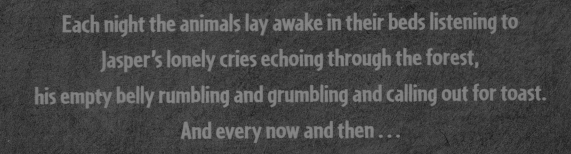

Each night the animals lay awake in their beds listening to
Jasper's lonely cries echoing through the forest,
his empty belly rumbling and grumbling and calling out for toast.
And every now and then . . .

"aaaaaa . . . aaaaaaa . . . tschoooooooooo!"

"Cooo . . . something has to be done . . .coooo!"

said the cuckoo one day.

Nobody could sleep, and besides, they all missed Jasper and wanted him back again.

"If only he could stop sneezing," said the red squirrel.

"But what can we do?"

"We know!" cried the dog twins excitedly.

"Why don't we take him to see the professor? He always knows what to do."

"Now that's a good idea!" they all agreed.

The next day they took Jasper to visit the professor.

He was a very wise owl who spent all his time reading big books and counting numbers.

"Mmmm . . . now let me . . . hooo . . . see . . . hooooo," he said.

First of all he measured Jasper from nose to tail.

"Oh, dear, much too . . . hooo . . . short . . . hooooo."

Then he inspected him through a magnifying glass.

"Oh, no, all the wrong . . . hoo . . . shade . . . hooooo."

Then he pinched him.

"Oh, my!"

Then he prodded him.

"Oh, my, my!"

Then he tickled him.

"aaaaaa . . . aaaaaaa . . . tschoooooooooo!"

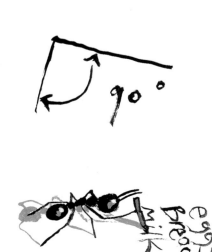

The flames roared from Jasper's nose and set the professor's hat on fire.

"Oh, my, my, my! Heee . . . eeeelp!" he yelled.

"Ooooops," said Jasper quietly.

"I have the solution!" declared the professor proudly, once the fire on his head had been put out.

"The poor wee beastie is suffering from . . . tickleyitis!

All the animals gasped in disbelief.

They had no idea what he was talking about.

But soon the professor was busy with balls of string and pieces of wood.
Then the sounds of hammering and sawing filled the morning air until at last . . .

stilts!

Poor Jasper was so tiny that the long grass had been tickling his nose and making him sneeze.
Now with his new long legs he could hunt for toast as much as he wanted—without setting fire
to things.